Rats!

SCHOLASTIC INC.
New York Toronto London Auckland Sydney

JANE CUTLER

Rats!

Pictures by TRACEY CAMPBELL PEARSON

ISBN 0-590-42064-X

Text copyright © 1996 by Jane Cutler. Illustrations copyright © 1996 by Tracey
Campbell Pearson. All rights reserved. Published by Scholastic Inc., 555 Broadway,
New York, NY 10012, by arrangement with Farrar, Straus and Giroux, Inc.
SCHOLASTIC and associated logos are trademarks and/or registered trademarks of
Scholastic Inc.

12 11 10 9 8 7 6 5 4 3 2 1   7 8 9/9 0 1 2/0

Printed in the U.S.A.   40

First Scholastic printing, October 1997

For Gabe Parker

Contents

Rats!

Wigged Out

"Swing!" cried Andrew Kelly. Edward Fraser swung—and missed. Andrew caught the softball and tossed it back to Edward's brother Jason, who was pitching. Andrew and Jason had decided to teach Edward to hit a ball before school started on Monday. They'd been working on it all week long.

Jason caught the ball and walked toward Andrew. "Time out," Andrew told Edward as he went to meet Jason.

"I don't get it," Jason said quietly to Andrew. "I'm throwing them as easy as I can."

"They're right over the plate," Andrew agreed, "and the perfect height."

3

Both boys went and stood by Edward. "Let's check your stance again," Andrew said.

"And your grip," added Jason.

Edward held the bat the way the older boys had taught him. He spread his legs wide enough to have good balance. He turned his head and peered toward the imaginary outfield.

"Now hold still," Andrew directed. He and Jason walked in a circle around Edward.

"Well, everything looks all right to me," Jason puzzled.

"Try putting your hands a little closer together," said Andrew. "And drop your left shoulder." Edward slid his left hand up on the bat. He dropped his shoulder. He squinted determinedly at the spot where the pitcher should be.

"Now try a practice swing," said Jason. He and Andrew moved out of the way.

Edward waggled the bat, getting ready. He put his weight onto his back foot. He waited for the imaginary ball to cross the plate—and then he swung, shifting his weight to his front foot and following through.

"Another home run!" he cried as he watched the imaginary ball soar over the trees near the end of the driveway. He tapped the plate with his bat. "How do I do it?"

"His form is almost perfect," Andrew said to Jason.

Jason nodded. "His swing is level, and he follows through," he said. "So why can't he ever hit the ball?"

Andrew shook his head. "We'll just have to keep at it," he decided.

Jason walked back to the pitcher's spot, which they'd marked on the driveway with white chalk. He eyed home plate, which was also made with chalk. He was pitching underhanded and slow. He couldn't make it any easier for Edward.

"Okay, Edward," he called, "here comes the pitch."

"Get ready," encouraged Andrew as he crouched down behind the plate.

Edward got ready. He glared at the pitcher. He tapped the plate with the bat. He adjusted his cap. He shuffled his feet. He put the bat in between his knees and wiped his hands on his pants. He picked up the bat again and took a practice swing.

"Edward!" Jason threatened.

"Ready!" answered Edward.

"Remember to keep your eyes on the ball," said Andrew.

Jason sent another perfect pitch toward the plate.

Edward kept his steady batter's eye on the ball as it came toward him, closer and closer.

When the ball got almost close enough to hit, Edward swung.

"Missed by a mile," grumbled Jason, who was tired of pitching.

"Eye on the you-know-what, now," Andrew patiently reminded Edward as he tossed the ball back to Jason.

Edward watched the white softball sail from Andrew to Jason. He kept his eyes on it the whole time. That part was easy. It was when the ball was coming at him that he couldn't stand to keep watching it. As the ball got closer and closer, his eyes shut all by themselves. Every time. But he swung anyway, as hard as he could, hoping that the bat and the ball would somehow connect, whether he was looking or not.

"Boys!" It was Mrs. Fraser, Edward and Jason's mother, coming down to the driveway with a page from the newspaper in her hand. "Back-to-school clothing sales are starting today. If we get to the mall right now, we might miss the crowds." She waved the newspaper in their direction.

"One more pitch?" Edward asked.

"Okay," she agreed, shading her eyes with her

hand so she could watch. "One more, and then we have to get going."

Edward got ready. Andrew crouched and pounded his fist in his mitt. Jason eyed the plate and released the ball.

Edward watched the white softball spinning lazily toward him. He kept his eyes right on it for as long as he could. But at the end he panicked, closed his eyes, and swung.

This time, to his surprise, Edward heard the solid, satisfying sound of the bat connecting with the ball! His eyes flew open. Jason and his mother had turned to watch the ball sail up into the trees at the end of the driveway. Andrew had stood up to watch it fly.

"All *right*!" Andrew exclaimed. "I knew you could do it!"

"Great hit," Jason called, starting to go after the ball.

"Amazing hit!" said Mrs. Fraser proudly. "I didn't think anyone could hit a baseball like that with his eyes closed!"

Jason stopped in his tracks. Andrew folded his arms across his chest, cocked his head to one side, and studied Edward. "Eyes closed?" he inquired.

Jason slowly walked toward Edward with his

hands on his hips, waiting to hear his brother's reply.

Edward turned his cap around backwards, the way he wore it when he wasn't playing ball. He scuffed the toe of his worn-out summer sneaker on the white-chalk home plate.

"Eyes closed?" said Jason.

"Closed?" echoed Andrew.

Edward dropped the bat and took off toward the back of the house. "Only at the end!" he called over his shoulder. "Only when the ball gets too close!"

"What did he say?" Jason asked.

"He said he only shuts his eyes at the end," said Andrew, sighing.

"Like, right before he swings?" asked Jason. Andrew nodded.

The two boys walked up the driveway to look for the ball. "He shuts his eyes," Andrew said, shaking his head in disbelief.

"I should have known it would be something like that," said Jason, "with Edward."

Edward didn't want to go shopping. He didn't care about what he wore. "I can just wear Jason's old stuff," he said.

"Edward, we've had this conversation before,"

his mother reminded him. "You can wear Jason's shirts, but you can't wear his pants. You and Jason have different shapes. His pants don't fit you. Jason and your cousin Alvin have almost exactly the same shape. That's why we send Alvin the pants Jason outgrows and buy new ones for you. Remember?"

Edward remembered. But he didn't think it was fair. Jason was his own brother. Why should Alvin be the same shape as Jason, and Edward be some other shape? Edward went into the bathroom and looked at himself in the full-length mirror. What was so different about his shape, anyway?

Jason came in to wash up. Edward stared at him.

"What are you staring at?" Jason wanted to know.

"You," answered Edward. "Your shape. What's different about it?"

"Nothing," said Jason. "There's nothing different about it. It's yours that's different."

"Who says?" demanded Edward.

"Mom says!"

"Mom says what?" asked Mrs. Fraser, coming to the door to see what was keeping them.

"That Edward's shape is different," explained Jason.

"Yes?" she asked.

"And I want to know what's the matter with my shape?" said Edward. "It looks all right to me."

"Of course it's all right," Mrs. Fraser said. "Just different from your brother's."

"And Alvin's," Edward reminded her.

"And Alvin's," she acknowledged. She looked at herself in the mirror and took a deep breath, pulling in her stomach as far as she could and shaking her head in dismay. "And mine," she added sadly. "Come on now, let's get to the mall before everyone else does."

The mall was crowded, but Mrs. Fraser said it wasn't as bad as she expected. "At least we found a parking space on the same planet as the store we want to go to," she pointed out.

The store she liked was a big, old-fashioned department store where she could find everything she needed to buy for the boys on one floor.

They took the elevator up and got out on 4, where a sign said, "Boys and Young Men's Department," and a huge banner read BACK-TO-SCHOOL SALE.

Jason and Edward trailed after their mother as she quickly gathered up packages of socks and underwear, the same kind they always wore, but in larger sizes than before. Then she said, "Okay, Edward first. What kind of pants do you want this year, Edward?"

11

"Same kind as last year," he replied.

"What colors?" she wanted to know.

"Same colors as last year," he answered.

"What size?" asked a salesman who had come to help the Frasers.

"We don't know," Mrs. Fraser said. "That's why I brought him with me."

The salesman whisked out a tape and measured Edward's waist and legs.

"Shirts?" the man asked.

"I wear my brother's old ones," Edward said.

The man turned to Jason. "Same clothes as last year but in a different size?" he asked, moving toward Jason with the tape measure.

Jason took a step backward. "No," he said, "I don't think so."

The man stopped in his tracks. Edward and Mrs. Fraser looked at Jason.

"What do you have in mind, Jason?" Mrs. Fraser asked.

"I'm not sure," Jason answered. He looked around at the tables overflowing with shirts, the racks bulging with different kinds of pants, the rows of jackets and sweaters and hats, the hundreds of square feet of "Boys and Young Men's Clothing." His expression was dreamy and peaceful. "Where's the beginning?" he wanted to know.

"The beginning?" asked the salesman.

"Yes," Jason said, "the beginning. I want to start at the beginning and end at the end. I want to see everything. And then I'll decide."

"Everything?" asked Mrs. Fraser, sounding faint.

"Everything," said Jason decisively. "So where is the beginning?"

For a few minutes, Edward walked along with Jason, his mother, and the salesman. Jason meant what he said. He wanted to see everything. He would be a fourth-grader in a couple of days, he reminded his mother, and would be playing on the upper playground with the fifth- and six-graders. He couldn't turn up looking wrong.

"No, of course you can't," his mother agreed. "Just take your time, and choose exactly what you want. We have all afternoon to shop."

The salesman excused himself. "I'll be nearby," he said, backing away. "If you need any help, just sing out."

Edward excused himself, too. "I'll be nearby," he said.

"Hold it right there," said Mrs. Fraser. "Where do you think you're going?"

"To the bathroom," Edward answered, thinking fast.

"And then where?" asked Mrs. Fraser suspiciously.

"Nowhere," Edward said. "I'll come right back and—and I'll sit over there and wait." He pointed to an empty couch in the shoe department.

His mother hesitated. "Look at this, Mom!" called Jason enthusiastically, holding up a huge pair of jeans that were torn nearly to shreds.

"Good grief!" cried Mrs. Fraser.

Edward saw she was distracted. He took advantage of the opportunity and sped away, in the general direction of the bathroom, which happened to take him past the escalator. He stopped to watch the Up escalator steps get smaller and smaller and disappear, one after another. He wondered where they went. Then he walked around to the other side of a wall and watched the Down escalator steps get bigger and bigger. He wondered where they came from.

When he got tired of watching escalator steps, he decided to take a ride on them. He rode down. He rode up. He rode down again. Then he got off.

He was on a different floor. He started to walk around to the up escalator side when he saw a small department he'd never seen before. It was like a little island with the escalator on one side and a wide aisle on the other. On the island stood tables, each one with a mirror attached to it. And on each table was a head made out of plastic. All the heads were covered with hair. But none of them had faces!

Edward sidled up to one of the tables. The faceless heads were all around him. He knew he shouldn't touch things, but his curiosity got the better of him. Gingerly, he reached out and touched a head with curly black hair, which startled him by slipping sideways!

Edward jumped. Then he looked more carefully. The hair was actually a wig. All the heads were wearing wigs. The Wig Department! he thought. He looked around. As luck would have it, he was all alone. He would begin at the beginning and try on every wig in the place.

Edward took off his baseball cap and put it on an empty head over in the corner. Then he tried on wigs. He tried on curly wigs and straight wigs, black, brown, red, gray, and blond wigs, short wigs and long wigs. He tried them on frontwards and he tried them on backwards, and every time he looked in the mirror he cracked up.

He spotted one that interested him more than the others. It was a yellow wig, with thick, sausage-like curls hanging down all around it and a lime-green bow on one side. Except for the color, it looked exactly like the hair on one of Emily Han's dolls, the one she brought to show-and-tell in kindergarten last year.

Edward carefully placed this wig on his head and looked in the mirror. He made faces at himself for a while and then he just stared. It was odd to have hair like a doll.

Just then Edward smelled something cooking, and he realized he was hungry. He wondered where the delicious smell could be coming from. He wondered what it was. And he wondered who would be allowed to cook in the middle of the store.

He followed his nose and found himself surrounded by glasses and dishes and silverware, by mixers and slicers and choppers, by pots and pans and bowls. He found himself standing right in front of a man dressed in a white apron and a white chef's cap, chopping meat and vegetables and stir-frying in a huge electric wok.

The chef worked quickly and dramatically, chopping, seasoning, tossing, stirring, all the while explaining what he was doing and making jokes with the crowd of shoppers who had stopped to watch him cook.

When he finished, he put the food into paper bowls with plastic forks and handed them around.

"Here you go, honey," he said to Edward, handing him a bowl full of spicy-smelling stir-fry.

"Thanks," said Edward, smiling.

"What a darling," someone behind Edward whispered to someone else. "Look at that beautiful curly hair."

Edward turned around to see who they were talking about. A large man at the back of the crowd was carrying a tiny white poodle. The poodle was not much of a dog, Edward thought, but it did have nice curly hair.

Edward ate while he walked, paying attention to his food and not to where he was going. When he looked up, he was in the toy department.

He threw away the empty paper bowl and the plastic fork, wiped his mouth on the sleeve of his T-shirt, and set about examining the wheeled toys. He checked out the bikes, the scooters, the unicycles, and the skateboards. Then he moved on and looked at the stilts and the pogo sticks. He tried the stilts, but he found out it was harder to walk on stilts than it looked. So he went on to a pogo stick. That was a cinch. Edward got the hang of it right away, and bounded off through the toy department, feeling like a kangaroo.

"Little girl!" someone called. "Little girl. Stop!"

Edward kept bouncing.

"I said stop!" the voice cried. "You're not allowed to do that!"

Edward stopped playing on the pogo stick. He glanced around the toy department to see what the girl was doing that was wrong. But he didn't see her. All he saw was a tall, nervous-looking salesman coming quickly toward him.

"Well," huffed the man, "are you quite finished?"

Edward thought for a moment. Then he noticed the racks of models and the building games. "Yes, I am, thanks," he said politely.

The salesman took the pogo stick and carried it back to where it belonged. Edward took down an erector set and opened the box. To his disappointment, all the pieces were inside plastic bags. He put it away and took down a box of Lincoln Logs. Happily, they were not in plastic. He dumped them out and sat on the floor to make something.

"Little girl!" came the exasperated cry.

Edward put away the logs and got up. Where was this little girl who was causing so much fuss, and what was she doing, anyway?

He went over to the counter where the dolls were displayed behind glass. Maybe she was looking at dolls.

The tall salesman appeared at Edward's side. "Now," he said, "that's more like it. You want to look at dolls. We have Barbie dolls and baby dolls, boy dolls and girl dolls, soft dolls and hard dolls, old-fashioned dolls and new ones that are anatomically correct." The man stared at Edward as if he had asked Edward a question and expected an answer.

Edward thought. "Anatomically correct?" he asked.

"Well," the man said. "On second thought, let's not worry about those. Unless your mother or father is here with you?" The man looked hopefully around.

"My mother is," Edward told him. "And my brother."

The man seemed relieved. "Good," he said.

"They're getting school clothes for my brother," Edward told him. "It takes a long time, because my brother has something the matter with his shape."

"That's too bad," the man said sympathetically. "Well, I'll tell you what. When your mother is finished taking care of your brother and his special needs, you bring her back over here and we can get out the anatomically correct dollies. Okay?"

Edward shrugged. "Okay," he said. "I guess."

"Fine," said the man, hovering over Edward to make sure he didn't play with anything on the way out of the toy department.

"Bye-bye," the man waved.

"Bye," Edward said. As he left, he looked around for the troublesome little girl, but he didn't see her.

Edward walked on, thinking it was time to get back to the Boys and Young Men's Department, and wondering which direction to go.

Suddenly a woman dressed in a princess costume stepped right in front of him. "Hello, there," she said, beaming down at him. Before he could reply, she sprayed him with something that smelled so awful he thought he would choke. "Baby's Breath," the woman announced gaily, spraying him some more. "A new perfume made especially for little girls. Do you like it?"

"No!" he cried, taking off.

Edward was in such a hurry to get away from the perfume lady he forgot about trying to find his way back. When he felt he was safe, he stopped running and looked around.

"Well," he heard someone say. "That child over there is just about the same size as my granddaughter."

"Excuse me," a saleslady said sweetly to Edward. "Would you mind helping us out here for a moment?" Edward hesitated. "Of course you wouldn't," she said, taking him firmly by the arm and leading him to a chair where a gray-haired woman sat holding a pile of frilly dresses in her lap.

"I'm trying to buy a dress as a surprise for my granddaughter," the woman explained to Edward. "And you're just about the same size as she is. Would you mind if we hold these dresses up in front of you, so I can get an idea of how they might look on her? There are so many pretty ones I just haven't been able to choose."

The saleswoman steered Edward to stand directly in front of the undecided grandmother. Then she said, "Pull up your pants legs, dear, and stand still."

Edward glanced around. He was trapped between the two women. He pulled up his pants legs and stood still. The grandmother held up a pale pink dress with an eyelet apron. "Hmmm," she said.

She held up a blue plaid dress with a white collar and white cuffs. "Mmmm," she said.

She held up a yellow dress with embroidery on the front.

She held up a dark green velvet dress with a lace collar.

Edward looked down. "This one!" he cried. "This is the best!"

21

"Do you think so?" asked the grandmother. "Is this the one you would want to have?"

Edward hesitated. He didn't want a dress. Still, if he had to have one, this was the one he would choose. "Yes," he said, "it is."

"No confusion in that answer!" said the saleslady happily.

"None at all," agreed the grandmother. "I'll take it." She handed over the green velvet dress. "Gift-wrapped, please," she said, opening her purse to get her wallet.

Edward slipped away. Behind him he heard the grandmother's voice. "Thank you," she called. "Thanks for your help!"

Edward hopped on one foot to roll down one side of his pants. He hopped on the other foot to roll down the other side of his pants. He looked up. There was the Down escalator. And getting onto it were his neighbors Marlene and Marilyn Conroy and their older sister, Janice.

"Hi!" he called, waving at the Conroys. They didn't wave back. They looked at him as if they didn't know who he was, and then they glided out of sight.

"I guess they didn't expect to see me here," Edward told himself, trying to understand why his friends would act as if they didn't know him.

He went around to the Up escalator. Just as he was about to step onto it, two teenagers pushed in front of him. One of the big bags they were carrying brushed against his head. Edward felt his baseball cap slipping off and grabbed for it and felt—fake hair.

Fake hair!

Edward gasped and grabbed the blond wig off his head. Then he ran as fast as he could, dodging shoppers and salespeople and mannequins and display tables and counters as he went. "Excuse me!" he cried over his shoulder to anyone or anything he bumped.

Finally, he skidded to a stop at the wig department, which was right where he'd left it, next to the Down escalator on the third floor.

Edward rolled his eyes up innocently and whistled to himself as he backed slowly in.

When he was surrounded and partly hidden by the tables and mirrors and heads and wigs, he looked frantically around. And there it was—his baseball cap—right where he'd left it.

Edward dashed over to the table in the corner, grabbed his cap, slapped it on his head, and turned it backwards. Then, carefully, he placed the wig he'd been wearing back where it belonged, and arranged the curls so nobody could tell it had even been touched, let alone worn all around the store.

Then Edward took the escalator up to "Boys and Young Men's" and sat on the couch in the shoe department to wait for his mother and brother.

They came almost right away, carrying mountains of packages. Mrs. Fraser sank down next to Edward.

"Whew!" she said.

Jason put down his packages and began looking at shoes.

"Is he going to begin at the beginning again?" Edward asked.

"I'm afraid he might," said Mrs. Fraser tiredly. She took off her cat's-eye glasses and closed her eyes for a few seconds. Then she got her second wind.

"Well," she said more brightly, sitting up straighter and putting her glasses back on. "You've certainly been patient today, Edward. As soon as we get you and Jason some shoes, I'll let you browse in the toy department for a while. As a reward."

"Oh, that's okay, Mom," Edward told her. "I wasn't patient so I would get a reward."

Mrs. Fraser looked surprised and pleased. "I

must say, Edward," she told him, "you never cease to amaze me."

But Jason, who had overheard, squinted at Edward suspiciously. And Edward had the feeling that his brother was not fooled.

Girl Trouble

Jason's third-grade teacher, Mr. Fortney, got promoted. Now he was Jason's fourth-grade teacher.

"I like that," Jason's father said. "It provides continuity."

"Continuity?" Edward asked, looking up from his drawing.

"Connection," his mother translated.

"You mean the fourth-graders are connected to Mr. Fortney?"

"I mean they already understand the way he teaches and the way he runs his classroom," she answered.

"They don't have so much to adjust to," put in his father.

Jason was silent.

"Right, Jason?" Mr. Fraser prompted. "No surprises. You already know the teacher and what he expects, so you can just dive right in."

"I guess," Jason said.

"Well, you do know Mr. Fortney already, don't you?" asked his father.

Jason sighed. "We sure do."

"So there's not as much to adjust to as there would be with a new teacher, right?"

"Right," Jason said glumly.

"I like my new teacher," Edward said.

"You liked your old teacher, too," remarked Jason.

"It's true," Edward agreed, smiling as he remembered his kindergarten teacher.

"Wait till you get Mr. Fortney," threatened Jason.

"I like Mr. Fortney," Edward told him. "I think he's funny."

Jason didn't respond.

"You liked Mr. Fortney last year, Jason," Mr. Fraser said. "Has he changed?"

Jason shrugged.

"He can't be all that different," his father reasoned, "after just one summer vacation."

"*Has* Mr. Fortney changed, Jason?" Edward asked,

carefully coloring sky around a jet he had zooming across the top of his picture.

"No, Mr. Fortney hasn't changed," Jason said. "But we've changed. At least, some of us have."

"Ah, the light dawns," said Mrs. Fraser. "What you're saying is, it would be better for some of you fourth-graders to have a new start with a new teacher."

Jason nodded yes.

"Maybe you could just change back," suggested Edward, coloring away.

Jason stared at Edward as if he were an alien from outer space. "Sure, Edward," he said. "Maybe we could all just shrink a couple of inches."

Edward thought about this. "You could slouch," he advised.

Mrs. Fraser broke in. "I think what Jason means, Edward, is that fourth-graders are different from third-graders in a lot of ways, not just size, and that Mr. Fortney is still thinking his students are exactly who they were last year."

"Right," Jason said. "He thinks if you were babyish last year, you still are. Or if you were shy last year, you'll be shy again. Or if you were smart last year, you're going to just love being in the gifted program and doing a gazillion extra dittos every single night."

"Mr. Fortney will figure it out," said Jason's father. "You kids have to be patient."

"After all," said Jason's mother, "Mr. Fortney taught third grade for years. This is his first time in the fourth grade.

"Teachers are human, too, Jason. Sometimes they need time to catch on to something new, just like anyone else."

"Gazillion extra dittos," Edward sang to himself, smiling.

"What's so funny?" Jason wanted to know.

"Funny?" asked Edward.

"You were smiling," said Jason.

"I was?"

"What were you smiling about?"

Edward looked puzzled. He had stopped paying attention to the conversation, and he didn't remember what had made him smile.

"Oh, something," he bluffed.

"What?" demanded Jason.

"Boys!" their parents warned.

One of the changes that had taken place between the third and the fourth grades had to do with teeth. Some of the kids in Jason's class had gotten braces. Jeffrey and Morley and Darius and Nicolette had them, and Lateesha was getting them.

Jeffrey and Morley and Darius were wearing black and orange gum under the metal parts of the braces, because the next holiday was Halloween. After Halloween, they planned to change to red and green, for Christmas. Nicolette was wearing purple, because purple was her favorite color.

"I wish I could get braces," Jason told his mother.

"When I was a kid, nobody wanted a mouth full of metal," his mother replied.

"It's not like that anymore, Mom," he explained. "It's neat now. Now the metal pieces go on top of this gummy stuff that comes in different colors. You can choose any color you want, and you can change it every month when you go in to have your braces adjusted."

"Colors?" his mother replied. "Gummy stuff?" She shook her head. "I think this is what they mean by the 'generation gap,' " she decided.

"More like the tooth gap," Jason informed her. "Some of my friends have enormous spaces between their teeth."

"Tooth gap," said Mrs. Fraser, chuckling. "That's a good one, Jason."

But Jason was not trying to be funny.

Another thing that had changed between third and fourth grade was the way the girls and boys in

31

Jason's class acted toward each other. Boys played only with boys. And the girls all stuck together. Even Alexandra Simpson, who was every bit as good a baseball player as Jason, never played ball with the boys anymore.

But it wasn't as if the girls just ignored the boys and left them alone. It wasn't nearly that simple.

One day, Lateesha passed a note to Jason when she was collecting the spelling papers.

Jason looked at the note and crammed it into his pocket. He showed it to his friends Lucas and Arnie and Morley and Jeffrey and Darius at lunch recess. "Look at this," he said, pulling out the crumpled note.

" 'Here are six names. Rate them according to how much you like them,' " Jeffrey read. " 'Alexandra Simpson, Elaine Abrams, Brittany Chan, Shawna Reeves, Lateesha Johnson, and Nicolette Savio.' "

"What should I do?" Jason asked his friends.

"You have to do what it says," Lucas advised. "You have to rate them."

"I do?"

"Yep," said Lucas. Lucas had an older brother and an older sister. He knew about these things.

"But I like them all the same," said Jason. Lucas and Jeffrey stared at him.

VOCABULARY
alveoli
atrium
bronchi
Capillaries
Cells

"You like them all?" Jeffrey said, sounding surprised.

"I mean, I dislike them all the same," Jason corrected himself.

"You don't like a single one of them?" Lucas asked.

"I mean, I haven't thought about it," stammered Jason.

Lucas sighed sympathetically. "Well, you have to think about it. It's part of what happens in the fourth grade. The girls always want to know things like that, so the boys have to think about it."

"We do?" Jeffrey asked.

Lucas nodded. "When you get a note like that, it's really rude not to answer it. My sister told me," he said, "and my sister knows about stuff like this."

"How rude is it?" Jason asked. He wasn't sure he would mind being slightly rude if he could get out of this.

"Really rude," said Lucas knowingly. "And they would get back at you, too."

"Get back at me?" Jason said. "That's silly. How could they get back at me?"

"They'd find a way," Lucas assured him. "When my sister was in the fourth grade, she and her friends got back at this boy by telling everyone he'd *kissed* a fifth-grade girl."

34

"Wow!" Morley said. "That's pretty mean."

Lucas nodded.

Jason looked at the list. "I'm going to have to think about this," he said, folding it and putting it into his pocket, carefully this time.

"I can help you rank them," Lucas offered.

Jason wondered how Lucas could help him decide how much he liked the girls. "That's okay, Luc," he said. "I'll do it myself."

Jason did his homework at the table in the family room. When he finished, he pulled out the list and stared at it. "What's that, Jason?" Edward wanted to know, looking with interest at the crumpled piece of paper.

"Girls' names," grumbled Jason.

"What for?"

"I have to rank them."

"What does that mean?"

"I have to say which one I like best, and then next best, and then next best. Like that."

"That's a funny thing to have to do," Edward said.

Jason went into his bedroom and closed the door.

He struggled over ranking the girls for a long time. Finally, he figured out what to do. He put Nicolette first. He liked Nicolette, he decided, because she was the kind of person who stuck with purple. He put Alexandra second, since he liked to play ball with her. After that, he put Elaine, since she lived nearby and they had gone to the same nursery school. In the number-four slot, he put Lateesha, Shawna, and Brittany, because he liked them all the same.

There, he thought. That's the end of that.

The next day, he passed his list to Lateesha. He felt relieved to be finished with ranking, and with girls. Now the girls would bother someone else. It was probably good, he told himself, that he'd been first, so he could get it over with.

But Jason was wrong. That was not the end of it. A few days later, Lateesha passed him another note. "Which two girls do you like best?" it said.

"This is ridiculous," he complained to Lucas. "I already ranked the six names. They could figure out that the top two names are the ones I like best."

"They could," Lucas agreed. Then he thought about it. "They probably just want to be sure."

"Sure of what?"

"Sure that you won't change your mind."

"Why would I change my mind?" demanded Jason. Lucas shrugged. "And what difference would it make if I did?"

"It would make a difference who you ended up going steady with," said Lucas.

"Going steady with!" exclaimed Jason. "I'm not going to end up going steady with anyone! Why are they doing this to me?"

"They must like you," Lucas said, grinning. "They must think you're cute."

"Cute!" fumed Jason.

"I advise complete cooperation," Lucas said.

Jason decided to take his advice. Nobody could make him go steady with anyone, after all. And if he answered this note, then the girls would probably leave him alone.

Besides, he had changed his mind. If they meant "like" instead of just like, then he would have to change the names around. He liked Nicolette and Alexandra and Elaine. But he "liked" Nicolette and Brittany. Numbers one and two.

He wrote down their names in order and gave the short list to Lateesha.

For a few days, nothing happened. Nobody passed any notes at all to Jason except for Morley, and his handwriting was so bad Jason couldn't read the note.

"What a relief," Jason thought to himself, "to be done with that!"

But he felt relieved too soon. On Monday afternoon, Lateesha gave him still another note. This time she didn't sneak it to him. She just marched right up, looked him in the eye, and cheerfully handed it over. Then she smiled at him, as if they were doing something fun together, and walked away.

This note said: "What do you rate Nicolette Savio, on a one-to-ten basis?"

Outraged, Jason caught up with Lucas and Jeffrey and Darius after school. "Now what am I supposed to do?" he cried.

Lucas read the note. "They want to know how much you like Nicolette. One is the lowest. And ten is the highest."

Jason had no idea how to answer. "If I put down ten, will they leave me alone?" he begged.

"Maybe," Lucas said.

"Maybe?" echoed Jason. "Could you ask your sister?"

Lucas said he would. "Call me up tonight," he told Jason. "I'll tell you what she says."

Jason waited until everyone in his house was busy. Edward was playing in the bathtub. Mr. Fraser was snoozing in his easy chair. Mrs. Fraser was making lists. "I have too much to do," she complained. "I keep saying yes when I should say no.

I'm completely overwhelmed. Making these lists helps me feel more organized."

Lists. Jason had decided he hated lists. But he didn't say this to his mother. Clearly, there were lists and lists.

When he was sure everyone was occupied and not paying any attention to him, Jason called Lucas.

"What did your sister say?" he asked.

"She said you have to go along to get along," Lucas replied.

"What does that mean?"

Lucas hesitated. "I think it means you better answer, or else," said Lucas.

"Thanks," Jason said, hanging up.

Jason couldn't write down 10. He didn't want the girls to think he believed Nicolette Savio was perfect. After all, nobody was perfect.

But when he thought about Nicolette, he couldn't think of anything he didn't like about her. She cracked good jokes, she was nice to people, she was interested in light-years, she wasn't afraid to try things, and she was, well, steady. She was the sort of girl who stuck with purple. Not perfect, maybe. But up near the top, Jason decided. 9, he wrote down. Then he added ½. 9 and ½.

Jason felt satisfied as he put the note into his backpack. He was sure Lateesha would show it to

Nicolette. That was fine with him. He didn't mind Nicolette knowing that he thought she was a 9½. Actually, he sort of liked the idea of her knowing it, as long as he didn't have to tell her so himself.

What did Nicolette think of him, he wondered. Did boys ever send notes to girls asking them to rate boys? He would have to check with Lucas.

For a few days, nothing more happened. I'm in the clear, thought Jason happily.

But he was wrong.

The first clue he had was when he saw Lateesha and Lucas pacing along at the far end of the playground. Their heads were close together, and they seemed to be talking seriously about something.

The second clue was when Lucas drew him aside after PE and whispered, "Meet me by the bike rack after school."

"Well?" Jason demanded, when he saw Lucas lounging against the fence near the bike rack later that afternoon.

Lucas held a finger to his lips and frowned at Jason. He beckoned with a jerk of his head, and the two boys sauntered away from the confusion of kids getting their bikes.

"What's up?" Jason wanted to know.

"The last step," Lucas replied.

"Last step?" asked Jason. "What are you talking about?"

"About you and Nicolette."

"Me and Nicolette?"

"About you asking Nicolette Savio to go steady."

"Asking Nicolette to go steady!" Jason shouted in alarm.

"Shhh," warned Lucas.

"Asking Nicolette to go steady!" Jason croaked.

"That's all you have to do," Lucas explained. "Then you're through."

"Through?" echoed Jason.

"Done. Finished."

"Finished with what?"

"With the girls."

Jason felt completely confused. "Let me get this straight," he said. "I ask Nicolette to go steady with me."

"Right," said Lucas. "And she accepts."

"She does? How do you know?"

"Trust me, Jason. She accepts."

"Okay, okay," said Jason. "I ask her to go steady with me, and she accepts." Lucas nodded yes. "And then what happens?"

"Nothing," Lucas said. "Except once in a while somebody might tease you and Nicolette about going steady."

"Yeah," said Jason suspiciously. "And what else?"

"Nothing else," Lucas assured him. "Really. Once you ask her to go steady with you and she accepts, you don't have anything more to do."

"Do I have to see her or talk to her or buy her stuff or take her with me anyplace?"

"Absolutely not!" said Lucas. "As a matter of fact, that would be very weird. After you two decide to go steady, then that's the end of it. You do that, and then you have nothing at all to do with each other. You're finished."

Jason was still doubtful. "Are you sure, Lucas?" he asked. "I don't want this to go on forever."

"I'm telling you, pal, I've checked it with my sister. You go steady, sometimes people tease you about it, and that's that. In the fourth grade, that's what 'going steady' means."

"Tease," Jason said to himself.

"No big deal," Lucas assured him. "Teasing is nothing. You can handle it."

"I know I can handle it," Jason agreed. "What I can't handle is any more of these notes, and this ranking and rating, and being bothered all the time."

"Well, that's what I'm trying to tell you," said Lucas. "All that will stop, just as soon as you ask Nicolette to go steady with you."

Jason took a deep breath. "Okay," he decided. "How do I do it?"

Lucas produced a piece of paper and a pencil from his backpack. "Just write down, 'Nicolette, will you go steady?' and sign your name."

Jason made Lucas turn around so he could lean on his back to write. "Now what?" he asked.

"Now put two boxes at the bottom of the page, one marked 'yes' and one marked 'no.' That way, all Nicolette has to do is check a box to answer."

Carefully, Jason drew the boxes. He handed the note to Lucas, who said he would give it to Lateesha. Lateesha would make sure that Nicolette got it. Nicolette would check 'yes.' She would give it back to Lateesha. Lateesha would pass it to Lucas. And Lucas would deliver it to Jason.

"How long is all this going to take?" Jason demanded.

Lucas shrugged. "It depends how long it takes for Nicolette to say yes."

"Well, what if she says no?"

Lucas looked blank. "I'm not sure," he answered. "She's supposed to say yes. If she says no, I'll talk to my sister."

Jason had to be satisfied with that.

• • •

Nicolette didn't say no. The smudged and wrinkled note came back to Jason the next day, with a check in the 'yes' box. Jason Fraser was going steady with Nicolette Savio.

"Way to go, Jason!" Arnie bellowed when he found out.

"Shhh," Jason commanded.

Nicolette looked over at them and grinned her purple grin. Jason felt himself getting red in the face. What he wouldn't have given, right at that moment, to have an overbite, or crowded teeth, or molars that wouldn't come down, or gaps, so he wouldn't have to smile back his ordinary, tooth-colored smile at the girl he was going steady with.

"Jason's got a girlfriend, Jason's got a girlfriend," sang Edward.

Jason squinted at Edward from across the family room and frowned a warning.

"A girlfriend?" asked Mrs. Fraser.

Edward saw the warning and got busy setting up the animals in his miniature zoo.

"Do you have a girlfriend, Jason?" Mrs. Fraser asked again, smiling at him and ducking her head so the rhinestones on her cat's-eye glasses twinkled in his direction.

"Of course not," Jason said quickly. Mrs. Fraser looked inquisitively at her son.

"No!" he shouted.

"No need to yell," she reminded him, as she left the room.

"Sorry," mumbled Jason. "Edward"—he turned to his brother—"don't you dare say that again."

"Say what?" asked Edward.

"That."

"What?"

"What you just said!"

"You mean, 'what?' "

"I mean—you know what I mean!" fumed Jason.

"Mmmm," Edward responded, turning back to his toys.

"Edward!" Jason warned.

"Jason!" Edward mimicked.

It was clear that Edward knew Jason was going steady, or he would never have dared to mimic him. Jason felt defeated. He slunk into his room and closed the door. If the first-graders knew about him and Nicolette, then everyone in the whole school knew. He had never felt so miserable.

At lunch on Saturday, Mrs. Fraser said that she'd met a very nice woman at one of her PTA committee meetings and had invited the woman and her husband to come over the next day, Sunday.

"We'll watch the football game and have an early dinner," she told Mr. Fraser. "They have one child, and I said it would be nice if she could come, too."

"She?" Jason said. "A girl?"

"How old is she?" asked Edward.

"About Jason's age," his mother answered.

"What are these people's names?" Mr. Fraser wanted to know.

"Sally and David Savio," answered Mrs. Fraser. "Their little girl is called Nicolette."

"Nicolette!" yelped Edward. Jason silenced him with a stern look.

"Pretty name, isn't it," Mrs. Fraser replied.

Edward gulped.

"Isn't it?" repeated his mother.

Edward tried not to snort.

"It's a very pretty name," Jason said, jumping in. "Right, Edward?"

Edward sputtered.

"Edward, are you choking on something?" Mr. Fraser asked. "Do you need a slap on the back?"

"I'll slap him on the back," Jason offered.

"No!" cried Edward. "I'm fine now. I just need a sip of water!"

Jason called Lucas. "The Savios are coming to my house for dinner tomorrow," he whispered urgently. "Ask your sister what I'm supposed to do now!"

"My sister's gone to be a counselor at Science Camp this weekend," Lucas replied.

"Ask your brother!"

"My brother's away at college," Lucas said. "You know that." In his panic, Jason had forgotten.

"Ask somebody!" he begged.

"Just calm down," Lucas advised. "And stay by the phone. I'll get back to you."

He called fifteen minutes later.

"Lateesha says Nicolette is just as upset as you are," he told Jason. "But there's nothing she can do about it. She told her mother she was sick, but her mother took her temperature and said she wasn't. So she has to come."

"Lucas, this is terrible!"

"It is," Lucas agreed.

"You told me if I asked Nicolette to go steady, I'd be finished!" accused Jason.

"How was I to know your mother would make friends with Mrs. Savio?" demanded Lucas. "Answer me that? How was I to know?"

Jason didn't respond.

"Don't go blaming this on me," Lucas said.

"I'm sorry, Lucas," Jason apologized. "I'm just upset."

"Well, quit acting like it's my fault," Lucas said. "I can't help it if girls think you're cute. I've done the best I can. You're on your own now." Lucas paused. "Lover boy," he teased. "Bye."

"Lover boy," Jason muttered.

"Lover boy?" asked Edward.

"You!" cried Jason.

"Mom!" hollered Edward.

"Boys!" their parents warned.

"Nicolette Savio is in my class at school," Jason told his mother miserably.

Mrs. Fraser was preparing food for Sunday dinner and getting out snacks for the football game.

"How nice, dear," she said distractedly.

"She has purple braces," Edward added.

"How nice, dear," his mother said. Then, "Purple braces?"

"On her teeth."

"Purple?"

"I told you, Mom," Jason reminded her. "A bunch of kids have colored stuff on their teeth now."

"Oh, yes," she said. "I remember." She shook her head. "Purple."

"She can change the color," Edward explained. "She doesn't have to keep purple. Lots of kids change every month."

"Not Nicolette," Jason said, sounding proud without meaning to. "Purple is her favorite color. She doesn't change."

His mother looked at him, no longer distracted. "She sounds like a strong-minded girl," Mrs. Fraser said.

"Well, she knows what she likes," Jason allowed.

"Yes," said his mother. "That's what I meant."

"When I get braces, I'm going to change every single month. I'm going to have different colors every chance I get," said Edward.

"You might not need braces, Edward," his mother reminded him.

Just then, the doorbell rang. It was the Savios. Mrs. Savio had brought a carrot cake. Mr. Savio had on a football jersey with the name of a college on it. Nicolette smiled so bashfully when she was introduced to the Frasers that her purple teeth didn't even show.

For a while, the three children sat in the living room with the grownups, watching the football game.

49

Edward got bored and turned a backwards somersault.

"Not in the living room, Edward," his mother reminded him. "If you want to play, go on down to the family room. Or outside. It's a beautiful day."

Edward stood up. "Want to play?" he asked Nicolette. She did. The two of them started out of the room.

"What about you, Jason?" asked his mother.

"I want to watch the game," Jason answered.

At halftime, Mr. Fraser suggested that Jason go and see how Edward and Nicolette were doing. Reluctantly, Jason got up. He went down the hallway to the family room and peeked in. Edward and Nicolette were playing Candy Land. Nicolette looked bored.

When she saw Jason, she grinned at him with all her purple teeth. "Football over?" she asked.

"Halftime," he answered.

"Nicolette and I are busy," Edward said. "We're playing Candy Land."

"Candy Land," scoffed Jason. "I bet Nicolette would rather play Ping-Pong, wouldn't you, Nicolette?"

She nodded yes.

"Me, too!" said Edward, jumping up. "Let's go out to the garage and play Ping-Pong."

"You and Nicolette play first," Jason suggested. "I'll play winners."

Even though she didn't play hard, Nicolette couldn't help beating Edward.

And even though she played as hard as she could, she had a tough time staying even with Jason.

Luckily, Nicolette knew how to put a lazy-looking spin on her serves that kept Jason from smashing them back at her every time. Plus she was left-handed, which sometimes seemed to confuse him.

For a while, Edward helped keep score. Then he got tired and wandered off.

Jason and Nicolette managed to stay tied four games in a row. After that, they stopped counting and just hit the ball back and forth while they talked.

As long as there were no parents around, Nicolette wasn't at all bashful, and she often grinned her purple grin at Jason. Every time she did, it reminded him of why he'd ranked her number one.

Ghosts

It was only the beginning of October, but already everyone had started thinking about Halloween. The two big windows of the One-Stop Party Shop had been decorated for the holiday. Jason and Edward walked down together to take a look at the display.

A tape concealed somewhere in the front of the shop was broadcasting scary sounds. As the boys approached, they heard the squeal of an old door creaking open, they heard the cackle of a witch, they heard the "Aaaah!" of a terrified person, they heard the clanking of chains, and they heard the "Oooooooooo" sounds of ghosts.

One window had been made to look like an old graveyard. Plastic headstones with RIP written on them leaned against one another. "R-I-P?" asked Edward.

"Rest in Peace," Jason explained.

Near the gravestones were big gray rubber rats with long sharp teeth, chewing on bloody entrails. Huge, hairy plastic spiders dangled on elastic bands, fake snakes slithered over everything, black bats were arranged so they seemed to swoop overhead, and white glow-in-the-dark skulls sat grinning here and there.

In the other window were skeleton masks and robber masks and witch masks and clown masks, pirate masks and ape masks and vampire masks, with costumes to match. On the floor of that window were beastly-looking fake hands and fake feet and tall bottles filled with watery red liquid and labeled "blood" and squat bottles filled with noxious green liquid and labeled "poison."

Both of the store windows dripped with dirty-looking cobwebs, and white ghosts with black circle eyes floated among them.

Edward looked carefully at everything. Then he went back to the graveyard window and studied the ferocious-looking rats. Edward's eyes were wide, and his face seemed a little pale.

"Same old stuff," said Jason. "Let's go."

But Edward wanted to look some more. "What's that bloody stuff the rats are eating, Jason?" he asked.

"Entrails," answered Jason. "Come on."

"What's 'entrails'?" Edward wanted to know.

"Guts," Jason said. "Entrails are guts. Let's go."

"Guts," Edward murmured as they started home. "Where do the rats get the guts to chew on, Jason?"

"They get them out of the dead bodies from the graveyard," Jason said. He saw that Edward was worried, so he lowered his voice to make it sound scary. "They get them out of dead bodies after someone digs up the bodies and doesn't bury them again. Then the rats sneak out and chew on the bloody guts of the corpses."

"Corpses," said Edward.

"Dead guys," explained Jason.

"I know. I was just saying it," said Edward.

They walked along in silence for almost a block. Jason was plotting. Edward was fretting.

"Why would someone dig up bodies and leave them around?" Edward asked finally.

"How should I know?" answered Jason.

"To steal the treasure that got buried with them by mistake?" suggested Edward.

"Probably," said Jason.

The two boys walked in silence for another half a block. Then Jason turned his head away from Edward and did his best ghost imitation: "Oooooo!"

"Ooooo, yourself," said Edward.

"What are you talking about?" Jason asked.

"I know that was you," Edward said.

"What was me?" asked Jason.

"That ghost sound you made was you," said Edward.

Just then, from behind them, the boys heard a long-drawn-out OOOOOOOO!

"Well, that wasn't me," Jason said.

"I know!" cried Edward, taking off.

Jason looked back. There were his friends Jeffrey and Morley standing on the sidewalk, laughing their heads off.

When Jason got home, he found his mother sitting at the dining-room table with a pencil and paper, making a list.

"Edward saw a ghost on the way home from the One-Stop," Mrs. Fraser told Jason.

"Heard a ghost," corrected Jason.

"Did you?"

"Did I what?"

"Did you hear a ghost, too?"

"Yep."

"What did it sound like?"

"Like a ghost. You know, OOOOOOOO!"

"Oh, that kind of ghost," said Mrs. Fraser. "You can come out now, Edward," she called. "The coast is clear."

Edward came cautiously out of the kitchen, where he had been hiding under a chair.

"It's the same ghost we always have around here at Halloween, Edward," Mrs. Fraser said. "A young ghost. A friendly one. Just practicing. Named Jason. Nothing to be afraid of."

"Named Jason?" Edward wondered.

"Yep," she said. "Same one we had last year, remember?"

Edward wasn't sure whether he remembered or not. "You know," his mother went on, "the ghost that says 'oooooo!' every once in a while but doesn't do anything else."

"Well, what else would you expect him to do?" Jason demanded.

Mrs. Fraser was studying her list. Edward meant to tell his mother that he had been walking with Jason when he heard the ghost noise, and that Jason hadn't made it. But he'd forgotten to.

"Well," Mrs. Fraser said, "an older, more experienced ghost might haunt, for example."

"Haunt?" asked Edward.

"Hang around all the time," his mother said.

"Playing tricks on people, and scaring them," Jason added.

"What kind of tricks?" Edward wanted to know.

"Make all the pictures hang crooked," Mrs. Fraser said, biting the eraser end of her pencil. "Make the milk turn sour. Move stuff from where you left it to someplace else. Like that."

"Or make your stuff disappear," Jason added. "Or make you disappear." He frowned meaningfully at Edward.

"But this ghost doesn't do any of those things," Mrs. Fraser pointed out. "This ghost just goes oooooo! and that's the end of it. Nothing to worry about from this ghost, Edward."

Edward brightened. "Yeah," he said happily. "Oooooo! is all this ghost can do. Who would be afraid of him, even if he isn't Jason?" He sat down next to his mother. "This ghost is just a wimp, isn't he?" he said.

"Or she," Mrs. Fraser automatically corrected.

Jason narrowed his eyes. "Oh," he said. "You can never tell. A ghost might be a wimp one year. But with some practice, that same ghost might be a lot of trouble the next year. I mean, if there is such a thing as a ghost, a ghost might find out it's more fun to haunt than just go oooooo."

"Is there such a thing as a ghost, Jason?" Edward asked.

"Naw, probably not. I've never seen one, anyway. Of course," he added as he left the room, "I don't hang around in the graveyard after dark, either."

Edward felt confused by Jason's reply. "Is there really such a thing as a ghost, Mom?" he asked.

"What's this about the graveyard after dark?" Mrs. Fraser wanted to know.

"When the rats gnaw on the entrails of the dead bodies and there's blood all over the place," Edward answered.

"Entrails," said his mother.

"That means guts," Edward explained.

"Yes," she agreed.

"So are there such things as ghosts, Mom?" Edward asked again.

Mrs. Fraser thought. "I don't think so," she decided.

"You don't think so?" Edward asked.

"I doubt there are," she said.

"You doubt there are?" he repeated.

"I've never seen one," she told him.

"Does that mean nobody else has?" he wanted to know.

"Probably."

"Probably?"

"Edward, you're going to have to discuss this with your father. I don't have time to talk to you about ghosts anymore. I'm the chairperson of the school's Halloween carnival this year, and I have mountains of stuff to do. I don't have time for discussions about ghosts or anything else. I have to be practical. I have to be disciplined." She gestured toward the list she had begun to write. "I have to make sure all the committees are staffed. I have to make sure the parents and the teachers participate. I have to organize everything, from A to Z—food, games, prizes. Everything. If you want to have philosophical conversations about ghosts, you will have to have them with your father."

When Edward's father came home from work that night, Edward met him at the door. "Dad," he asked, "are there such things as ghosts?"

"Of course not," his father said.

But there were other opinions.

Elaine Abrams reported that she and her cousin visited her grandmother and slept in the room that her dead grandfather had used as his study. His rocking chair was still there. During the night, Elaine said, she was awakened by the creak-creak sound the chair made when someone rocked in it. She opened her eyes, and sure enough, the chair was rocking back and forth, the way it had when her grandfather sat in it, reading a book or listening to music.

"Rocking back and forth?" Edward asked in a hushed voice.

Elaine nodded. "Just the way it did when he sat in it," she repeated.

"What'd you do?" asked Edward, wide-eyed.

"I watched it rock for a while," she said. "And then I went back to sleep."

"And in the morning?" asked Edward.

"In the morning, it was just sitting there," Elaine answered.

"Who saw the empty chair rocking except you?" Jason challenged.

"Nobody," said Elaine.

"You didn't wake up your cousin?" Elaine shook her head no. "So you have no corroboration of your story."

"What's 'corroboration'?" asked Edward.

"He means nobody else can say they saw what I saw," Elaine explained.

"Right," Jason said.

"But that doesn't matter. I did see it. And I watched the chair rocking for a long time before I went back to sleep. And even after I closed my eyes, I could hear the creak-creak. I know Granddad was there in his rocking chair."

"Maybe," said Jason.

"I know he was, too, Jason," Edward said. "How else could you explain it?"

"Elaine could have dreamed it," Jason said.

"But I didn't," said Elaine.

"See, she didn't," Edward said.

"It would be more believable if your cousin saw it, too," Jason said.

"Yes, it would," Elaine agreed. "If it happens again, I'll wake her up."

Alexander Friedman came over. He was wearing an arrow with the pointy end coming out one side of his head and the feathered side coming out the other. The curved, plastic piece that held them together was hidden under his baseball cap. He looked as if he'd been shot through the head with a red plastic arrow. Stuck in his belt he had a real-looking plastic knife with a retractable blade.

Before anyone even had a chance to say hi to him, Alexander stuck himself in the chest with the fake knife and fell down, spilling bright red plastic blood out of his pocket onto the floor. Then he flopped over on his back and played dead.

Alexander had spent his whole month's allowance at the One-Stop.

"Neat-o!" said Edward.

"Get up, Alexander," said Jason.

"Can I see the knife?" Elaine asked. Alexander sat up and handed it to her. Edward liked the way the arrow looked. "How much did that arrow cost?" he wanted to know.

"Two-fifty," said Alexander. "But it was worth it."

Edward agreed. Later he would have to get Jason to help him empty out his bank and count his money. He might have enough for an arrow like that.

"Do you believe in ghosts?" Edward asked Alexander.

"Not really," said Alexander.

"Not really?" Edward wanted to know.

"No," Alexander decided. "I don't."

"Elaine saw a ghost," Edward told him eagerly. "She saw her granddad's ghost sitting rocking in his rocking chair one night."

"You did?" Alexander asked Elaine.

"Well, I saw the chair rocking," Elaine explained, "all by itself. And it was Granddad's room and it was Granddad's chair."

"And he was dead?" Alexander said.

"Yep," Elaine said.

Alexander thought about this. "That's amazing, Elaine," he said. "I guess I do believe in ghosts, if you saw one."

"But she's the only person who saw it," protested Jason. "She's got no corroboration. She was the only witness."

Alexander thought some more. "But Elaine doesn't ever lie," he said to Jason. "Everyone knows that."

Elaine nodded and crossed her arms. She had a reputation for honesty, and she was proud of it. She didn't even believe in telling white lies, no matter how harmless and convenient they might be.

"Maybe she was dreaming," countered Jason.

"But she said she woke up," Edward argued.

"I did wake up," Elaine said.

"If she woke up, she couldn't have been dreaming," reasoned Alexander.

"So you think she saw a ghost," said Jason.

Alexander nodded. "I do."

"Even though you didn't believe in ghosts five minutes ago."

"Yep," said Alexander pleasantly. "I changed my mind. Now I believe in ghosts."

"That was quick," grumbled Jason.

"Well, what difference does it make?" Alexander wanted to know. "Let's go play."

Andrew Kelly wasn't interested in ghosts. He was interested in vampires. "I mean, you're going to know if you run into a ghost, and what can they do to you, anyway? They're dead. But a vampire is different."

"How different?" Edward asked.

"A vampire has a human form in the daytime," confided Andrew, "and becomes a vampire at night. That's when he drinks human blood and all."

"Where does he get the blood from?" asked Edward.

"From somebody's neck," said Andrew.

"And what happens to the guy whose blood the vampire drinks?" Edward wanted to know.

"That guy dies and then becomes a vampire, too," said Andrew. "And anybody could be a vampire," he added. "You can't tell who they are, in the daylight."

"I could be a vampire, Edward," Jason said.

"But I've seen you at night, Jason," Edward countered. "And the only thing you suck on is your toothbrush."

"Yeah, he's one of those special vampires who lives on toothbrush juice," Andrew said, laughing.

Ghosts, werewolves, witches, skeletons, pirates, vampires, superheroes. Every kid in the neighborhood was trying to decide what to be for Halloween.

"We're all going to be tramps," Jason announced.

"All?" asked his mother.

"All the boys in the fourth grade," he answered. "We're going to hang around together and be tramps."

"All for one and one for all," she said distractedly.

"No, tramps," he corrected her. "That's pirates."

"Right," she said.

"My friend Betsy is going to be a pirate," Edward said. "She's going to wear a black eye patch and a fake hook for a hand and she's going to carry her tame parakeet on her shoulder for a parrot. She's calling herself Captain Bones. It's a pirate name she read in a book."

"That sounds like a good costume," Mrs. Fraser said.

"So what are you going to be?" Mr. Fraser asked Edward.

"A ghost," Edward told him. "In a white sheet. Saying *oooooo!*"

"I'm going to be a gypsy fortune-teller," said Mrs. Fraser. "I have to be. I can't get anybody else to work the gypsy fortune-telling tent."

"What about you, Dad?" asked Jason.

"I'm going to help at the dunk-the-teacher booth," said Mr. Fraser. "I'm going to dress up like an old-fashioned carnival barker and give out the balls for people to throw. And if anyone happens to throw a ball that hits the spot, I'm going to throw the switch that dunks the teacher in the plastic pool of water. And then I'm going to fish him out."

"Him or her," Edward reminded his father.

"No, it's him," his father said. "It's going to be Mr. Fortney on the dunking plank this year. Him. Dressed up as a lady clown."

"Nobody ever hits the spot, anyway," Jason complained. "They make it small."

"It's just as well," his father said. "Would you like to be the one to dunk Mr. Fortney?"

"Good point," Jason admitted.

One week before Halloween, Marlene and Marilyn Conroy turned the shed in their back yard into a haunted house. They put flyers in everyone's mailbox. Jason read the flyer to Edward. "Only 50 cents to go through the scariest haunted house in the universe!" the flyer said. "Second time around, only 25 cents. If you make it out alive, that is."

"Shrunken heads!" the flyer proclaimed. "Loose

eyeballs! Brains in a bucket! And a rocking chair that rocks all by itself! Come one, come all!"

"Fifty cents," Edward said. "That's pretty good."

"If you spend fifty cents to go to the Conroys' haunted house, you won't have enough money for that plastic arrow," Jason reminded him.

"I don't care," Edward decided. "I'm going to the haunted house!"

"Have fun," Jason said.

"Aren't you coming, Jason?"

"Nope."

"Don't you want to see the shrunken heads?"

"You can tell me about them," Jason said. "I'm saving my money for the Halloween carnival at school Friday night. My friends and I are going to try every single thing."

"Even throwing the ball to dunk Mr. Fortney?"

"Especially throwing the ball to dunk Mr. Fortney!"

"Wow!" said Edward as he went to his room to get fifty cents.

The sounds of cries and moans came from the Conroys' shed. Marilyn was standing by the door, collecting money. She was dressed as a witch. Marlene was nowhere to be seen.

69

"Step right up, my dearie," croaked Marilyn in a witch voice.

"Am I the only one here?" Edward hesitated.

"Right now you are, except for Alexander. He's inside already," Marilyn said, in her own voice. "So step right up, Edward."

She reached out her bony witch's hand to grab Edward, but he jumped back. Someone turned up the sound of cries and moans and added the sound of a clanking chain. "Oooooo!" another voice groaned, somewhere inside the shed.

"Let me out! Let me out!" It was Alexander Friedman. He tore out of the shed and sped away, screaming.

"Now it's your turn, my pet," croaked Marilyn, and she grabbed Edward's arm and twisted his wrist a little until he gave her his two quarters.

Then she shoved him into the pitch-dark shed.

The floor under his feet was soft and rubbery. A shiny skull floated up near the ceiling. Something webby brushed against his face. He heard rats gnawing. He heard the creak-creak of a rocking chair. Suddenly a red light went on, and he saw another witch bending over a smoking cauldron. On the shelf behind her, he saw tiny human heads, no bigger than apples. The witch had a long nose

and green skin and she cackled when she saw him and beckoned him with a bony green finger.

"Come here," she croaked. "Give me your hands."

Edward was afraid not to do what he was told. He held out his hands. Suddenly the light went off again! His left hand was plunged into a bucket of cold slimy stuff.

"What's that?" he cried.

"Brains!" croaked the second witch.

Then she grabbed his other hand. "And these," she said, pushing his fingers into a bowl of small, round, slippery things, "are *eyeballs!*"

The red light went on and off, and the witch cackled horribly. "Let me out!" Edward started to cry. "Let me out!"

"Edward!" said the witch, in Marlene Conroy's voice, "are you pretending?"

"Let me out!"

The shed door opened. "What's going on?" the other witch asked, in Marilyn Conroy's voice.

"Turn on the light," said the Marlene-witch.

The Marilyn-witch turned on the light. Then both witches took off their witch masks and their pointy hats.

Edward snuffled and wiped his face with his hands.

"You don't have to be scared, Edward," Marlene said. "It's all just fake."

Edward snuffled some more. "I want to go home," he said in a small voice.

"You can go home," Marilyn said, pointing to the open door of the shed. "But don't you want to stop crying first?"

Edward did.

"Sit down for a minute," Marlene advised, taking a skull and some snakes off a stool and pulling it forward for Edward to sit on.

"It's all fake," Marlene said again. But Edward was still snuffling. He couldn't help it.

"Look," Marilyn said. "Look, Edward, here's the tape recorder with the scary-sounds tape on it. We've been working on it for a month." She turned the machine on, but was careful to keep it soft. Edward heard little moans and cries. He heard tiny ooooooo's. He heard the creak-creak of a teensy rocking chair.

Then the girls showed Edward how they worked the lights. They showed him the piece of dry ice smoking inside their mother's biggest soup pot.

"But what about the shrunken heads?" Edward sniffled.

"Shriveled old apples with faces painted on." The girls showed him one.

"And the brains in the bucket?"

"Just spaghetti!" they said. "Cold spaghetti!"

"And the eyeballs?" Edward asked, slyly snuffling another time or two.

"Peeled grapes!" the girls announced. "See?" They held the proof out so he could see.

"All fake," Edward remarked.

The Conroys nodded eagerly. "All fake!" they said. "Nothing in the world to be afraid of. Honest."

"I want my fifty cents back," Edward said.

"You what?" exclaimed the Conroys.

"I want my fifty cents back," Edward told them. "This was all a big fake. I shouldn't have to pay fifty cents to go through a fake haunted house. I wouldn't have paid you anything if I'd've known it was all fake."

Marlene and Marilyn had a quick conference.

They came over to Edward. One stood on one side of the stool. One stood on the other.

Edward looked up at Marilyn. He looked up at Marlene. They looked down at him. "Marilyn," Marlene said sweetly, "why do people come to haunted houses around Halloween?"

"Why, Marlene," Marilyn said, just as sweetly, "I think they come to haunted houses to get scared."

"What do you think, Edward?" asked Marlene.

"I think so, too," Edward agreed.

"You think people pay fifty cents to come to a haunted house to get scared?" Marilyn asked very, very sweetly.

"Yes," Edward said. "I think so."

"And were you scared, Edward?" asked sweet, sweet Marlene, bending over to look into Edward's face.

"You *were* scared, Edward," said sweet, sweet Marilyn.

They had him. He nodded.

"Say it," said Marlene in her normal voice, putting her witch mask on.

"Say it," said Marilyn in *her* normal voice, putting her witch mask and her witch hat on.

"I was scared," Edward said.

"So you don't get your fifty cents back, right?"

"I guess," said Edward.

"I mean, a deal's a deal, isn't it, Edward?" Marilyn asked.

"I guess," said Edward.

"Good," said Marlene, her voice muffled behind her mask, as she led Edward to the door of the shed. "So we don't owe you fifty cents. You got scared, which is exactly what you paid for."

Edward stepped out of the witch's shed into the

Conroys' back yard. "What if I tell?" he said, turning to face the two witches. "What if I tell everybody everything?"

"Tell?" asked Marilyn.

"Tell?" asked Marlene.

"Yes, tell," said Edward. "About the dry ice and the shriveled apples and the tape and the cold spaghetti and the peeled grapes."

The Marlene-witch took a step forward. "What if *we* tell?" she asked.

"Tell what?" Edward wanted to know.

"Tell that you got so scared you cried and cried," explained the Marilyn-witch.

"You wouldn't!" said Edward.

"Of course we wouldn't," the witches promised.

"And you wouldn't," the witches said.

"Of course I wouldn't," Edward promised.

Several children came in through the back-yard gate. They lined up in front of the shed. The tape of scary sounds started to play loudly.

"Step right up, my dearies," the first witch croaked to the new customers.

And then Alexander Friedman tore out of the shed. "Let me out! Let me out!" he cried, and sped away, screaming.

Rats!

"I bet you're not allergic to rats," Rudy Murata insisted.

"We're allergic to everything," Jason assured him.

"Everything," Edward agreed sadly.

"But rats don't shed," Rudy argued. "Rats don't have dander. Rats don't smell. And they're real smart. And a lot of fun. And hardly any trouble at all. Honest."

Rudy's female rat, Katherine, had had babies. A litter of seven! It was Rudy's responsibility to find homes for them.

"You might not be able to find homes for all of them," Edward said.

"You could give the extras to a pet store, for

free, and then they could sell them and make a profit," Jason suggested.

"Baby rats are sort of like kittens, Jason," Rudy said.

"Playful and cute," said Edward, nodding.

"Too plentiful and hard to get rid of," corrected Rudy.

"Plentiful?" asked Edward.

"Too many of them," Jason explained. "More baby rats than people who want them."

"But if I can't find homes for them, then I *will* take them to the pet store," Rudy said. "Mr. Clark will give me a dollar for every baby rat I bring him."

"A dollar!" exclaimed Edward.

"Then what's the problem?" asked Jason.

"The problem is that after they grow a little bigger, he'll use them for snake food."

"Snake food?" said Edward.

"Yep," Rudy said, imitating a snake gulping down a half-grown rat. "Down the hatch."

"What kind of snakes eat whole rats?" Jason wanted to know.

"Different kinds," said Rudy. "At Mr. Clark's, he feeds them to the boa constrictor."

"So if you can't find homes for Katherine's babies, they're boa brunch," said Jason.

"Boa brunch," said Edward, giggling.

"Not funny," said Rudy, giving Edward a poke. "How would you like it if Katherine's babies were yours and got fed to a boa?"

"I wouldn't like it," Edward admitted.

"Look," said Jason, "the only way to approach this problem is scientifically. If it turns out that Edward and I aren't allergic to rats, then we'll see if our parents will let us take two of Katherine's babies off your hands. If we are allergic, no deal."

"My back is to the wall," Rudy agreed. "Everybody I know except the two of you have some sort of pet already."

"What's 'scientifically'?" Edward wanted to know.

"We'll conduct a controlled experiment," Jason explained. "We'll repeat it over and over. We'll prove whether we are or are not allergic to pet rats."

"Mr. Fortney might even be willing to give us extra science credit for the experiment," said Rudy.

"Good thinking, Rudy," said Jason. "At least we won't be wasting our time."

"And maybe we could even end up getting pets," said Edward.

Jason designed the experiment. He and Edward would go over to Rudy's house after school. Before they went into the room with the rats or took the rats out of their cages to play with them, Jason would write down any allergic symptoms they were already having.

For the first part of the experiment, they would just sit in the room with the rats in their cages. That way, the boys would find out if they were allergic to the pine chips in the bottoms of the cages or to the rodent mix the rats ate.

If they showed no signs of sniffles, sneezes, rashes, itches, hives, or any other allergic symptoms, they would go on to part two of the experiment the next day. They would take Katherine out of her cage and play with her.

If they showed no signs of allergies after they played with Katherine, they would come back the next day and each choose their favorite baby rat and play with it.

If they still showed not a single sign of allergy, Jason and Edward would know that they were not allergic to rats. Then they would present the results of the experiment to their parents and try to persuade them to allow the boys to adopt two of Rudy's rats.

Jason knew exactly what approach to use. To their mother, he would explain that if they personally did not adopt the rats, the babies would have to be turned over to that monster, Mr. Clark, at the pet store, who would fatten them up and feed them to his snake.

To their father, he would point out how having pet rats would help him and Edward learn to be more responsible. How it would make them more thoughtful and mature if they had someone beside themselves to look after.

"It'll be a cinch," Rudy encouraged. "Your parents will never be able to resist those arguments."

"Never!" agreed Edward. "And then we'll have pet rats!"

"Only if we aren't allergic to them," Jason reminded his brother. "Allergies, remember?"

"I'm sure I'm not allergic to them," Edward said. "I can tell I'm not going to be."

"Unfortunately, that's not quite good enough," Jason told Edward. "*I* have to be not allergic to them, too."

"Oh, right," said Edward. He had forgotten about that part.

"When does the experiment begin?" Rudy wanted to know. He had seven four-week-old rats to unload. He wanted to get started.

"We'll be over after school tomorrow," promised Jason.

. . .

The next day, Jason and Edward and Rudy went to Rudy's after school. "Any allergic symptoms today?" Jason asked Edward as they walked along. Edward thought. "Come on, Edward," Jason said. "You have to be honest or it will mess up the experiment."

Edward thought some more. "Runny nose?" coached Jason. "Itchy eyes? Scratchy throat?"

The minute Jason said "runny nose," Edward snuffled. When Jason said "itchy eyes," Edward squinched. And when Jason said "scratchy throat," Edward had to clear his throat two or three times.

"Edward, stop that," Jason warned.

"Stop what?"

"Stop having every allergic symptom I mention, whether you have it or not."

"Then stop mentioning symptoms," Edward said, "so I can stop having them."

When the boys got to Rudy's, they went to his bedroom, where he kept his rat cages and his rats. Katherine and her babies had a big cage of their own. Rudy's other rat, Clifford, had a cage of his own. Both cages were made of wire, with pine chips on the bottom, dishes of rodent mix in the corners, and water bottles suspended from the sides at just the right height for the rats to stand up and drink out of.

Katherine was a hooded rat, Rudy explained, which meant she had a brown head and a white body. Clifford was white. The baby rats were all mixed up. Three were pure white, like their father. Two were brown. One was hooded, like Katherine. And one was spotted brown and white.

It was time for the experiment to start. Jason and Edward sat down on Rudy's bed, across the room from the shelves that held the cages. Rudy closed the bedroom door and sat down, too.

"Fifteen minutes," said Jason.

"Check," said Rudy, looking at his watch.

"That's a long time, just to sit here," said Edward, restlessly swinging his legs.

At the end of fifteen minutes, Jason pulled out a notebook and pencil so he could record the first day's results. "I'm not going to name any symptoms," he said, glancing meaningfully at Edward. "Just tell me if you feel allergic."

"Nope," said Edward.

"No symptoms?"

"Nope, none."

"Me, neither," said Jason. He wrote down the results of the first day's experiment. No allergic symptoms caused by sitting in a room with rats in their cages.

"Achoo!" sneezed Rudy, whose nose had started to tickle. "Achoo!"

The next day after school, the boys went back to Rudy's. This time, Rudy took Katherine out of her cage and let her run around on his bed. Then he picked her up and handed her to Jason.

Jason played with her for five minutes. Then he handed her to Edward, and Edward played with her for five minutes, too. After that, Rudy put Katherine back into her cage.

"Any symptoms?" Jason asked.

"Nope," said Edward, smiling. "None."

"Me, neither," Jason said. He wrote down the results of the second day's experiment. No allergic symptoms caused by playing with a grownup rat.

"Great," said Rudy, rubbing his itchy eyes.

The next day after school, Jason and Edward went to Rudy's again. This time, each boy chose the baby rat he liked best. Edward chose the brown-and-white one. Jason chose one that was pure white.

The boys played with the babies for fifteen minutes and then put them back in the cage with their mother.

"Any symptoms?" Rudy asked.

"Nope," replied Jason and Edward.

"Terrific!" said Rudy, clearing his scratchy throat a couple of times.

· · ·

Mr. and Mrs. Fraser listened carefully to Jason and Edward's request. They both liked the way the boys had planned and carried out a scientific experiment. Mrs. Fraser was upset when she heard that Katherine's babies might become brunch for a boa. Mr. Fraser was glad when he found out that his sons wanted to take on more responsibility.

Convincing Mr. and Mrs. Fraser turned out to be a cinch, just as Jason had predicted. But there were a few things Mr. and Mrs. Fraser insisted on that the boys hadn't predicted.

First, there was to be a trial period of one month. If either boy seemed to become allergic during the first month they had pet rats, Rudy would have to take them back.

Second, the boys would have to buy cages, food, pine chips, and water bottles themselves, out of their own savings.

And third, Jason and Edward had to be sure they got either two females or two males, so they wouldn't end up with a litter of baby rats of their own that they would have to find homes for.

"That's easy," Rudy told Jason and Edward when he gave them two old cages he wasn't using and a couple of extra water bottles he had, too. "All these babies are female, so there can't be any problem."

"All of them?" Jason asked.

"Every single one," Rudy assured him. "I can tell. I've had rats for a long time. This is Katherine's third litter, you know."

"How can you tell?" Edward wanted to know.

"Duh, just look, Edward," Rudy said.

"Yeah," said Jason.

Edward peered at the baby rats. "They all look the same to me," he said.

"That's my point," said Rudy. "They all look the same, because they all are the same. They're all female. If you check out Clifford, you'll see he's different. He's male."

Edward twisted and turned so he could get a good look at the back end of Clifford. Clifford didn't seem to like Edward looking at him that way. He kept moving around so that his head was always facing Edward. Edward kept turning and twisting and trying to see. Clifford kept being too quick for him. Edward decided to fake it.

"Oh, yeah," he said, "Clifford's a male, all right."

Rudy and Jason nodded.

"The babies are all female," Edward told his mother when he and Jason had finished setting up their cages side by side on a shelf in the family room.

"So there isn't really any reason we have to keep

them in separate cages," Jason added. "We could let them share one cage sometimes so they can play together."

Mrs. Fraser said she would think it over. But Mr. Fraser said no, no sharing cages for now. They would wait until the rats were bigger so they could be absolutely sure Rudy hadn't made a mistake.

"But Rudy knows all about rats," Jason argued. "This is his third litter. And he says they're all female."

"It's his third litter," Edward repeated. "He knows."

"It's Katherine's third litter," Mr. Fraser corrected. "And I imagine Rudy does know how to tell if a rat is male or female. But I called Mr. Clark at the pet store, just to make sure, and he said to wait a couple of weeks before you let them live together, just to be on the safe side."

"Which side is the safe side?" wondered Edward.

"Just to be sure," explained Mrs. Fraser.

"Well, they've been living together all this time, in the same cage as their mother," Jason pointed out.

"Good thinking, Jason," his father said. "You have a good head on your shoulders. But up to now they've been too young to mate, so it hasn't been a danger. Now that they're older, we need to be more careful. Mr. Clark said that after they're about nine weeks old, we'll be able to tell for sure. Then they can play together all they like. If they're really both female, that is."

"Dad," Edward said, "Jason's head isn't on his shoulders."

Mr. Fraser looked inquiringly at Edward.

"You said Jason has his head on his shoulders. But look, his head is right on his neck, just like everybody else's," Edward explained.

"Right," agreed Mr. Fraser. "Of course. It's just an expression. A way of saying that he has a good brain."

"On his neck," Edward insisted.

"Inside his skull, actually," said Mrs. Fraser.

"Protected by his cranium," said Mr. Fraser, smiling.

"The head bone connected to the neck bone . . ." sang Mrs. Fraser.

"The neck bone connected to the shoulder bone . . ." sang Mr. Fraser.

"The shoulder bone connected to the arm bone . . ." sang Mrs. Fraser.

"The arm bone connected to the wrist bone . . ." they sang together. "The wrist bone connected to the hand bones, the hand bones connected to the finger bones . . ."

"Oh, bones, them bones, them dry bones!" sang Mr. and Mrs. Fraser, laughing as they pranced arm in arm out of the family room.

Edward shrugged. Jason shook his head. They could hear their parents singing as they went through the house, their voices growing fainter: "The foot bone connected to the ankle bone . . . the ankle bone connected to the shin bone . . . the shin bone connected to the knee bone . . ."

Jason shrugged. Edward shook his head. They took their rats out of the cages and sat down on the couch to play with them. It was important to handle pet rats, if you wanted them to be tame.

Each boy watched his rat carefully, to see what its personality was like. They wanted to give them names that fit.

Jason thought his rat was gentle and sweet. He named her Rose.

Edward thought his rat seemed tough and adventurous. He named her Spike.

"Spike is not a girl's name," Jason informed Edward.

"It is now," Edward pointed out.

Rose and Spike lived side by side, each in her own cage. Often they stood on their hind legs and faced each other through the wire mesh, sniffing and seeming to want to play.

"How long do we have to keep them apart?" Edward asked.

"Dad says until they're nine weeks old," Jason reminded him.

"That's three more weeks," complained Edward.

"Yep," Jason answered. He was on his way to soccer practice, and he didn't have time for a discussion.

"But they want to play together now," Edward said.

"Yep," Jason answered. "Have you seen my goalie shirt?"

"Not this week," Edward told him.

Jason went to see if the shirt was still in the laundry hamper. It was. He put it on.

"Want to come watch my practice?" Jason asked Edward. Edward shook his head no. Even though most of Edward's friends were already playing soccer, Edward had decided to wait at least another year. He had been to a lot of Jason's soccer games and watched the kids standing around kicking one another. It didn't look like fun to him.

After Jason left, Edward played with Spike for a while. He played with Rose. Then he put them back into their cages and got fresh food and water for each of them.

By the time the baby rats were nine weeks old, it was clear that they would never be able to play together. Spike was a female rat, as Rudy had said. But Rose turned out to be a male.

Edward felt terrible. He knew Rose and Spike were disappointed. He knew they'd been counting on sharing a cage and keeping each other company. Besides, he had promised them.

"I bet Rose and Spike hate me," he told his mother.

"Mmmm?" she wondered.

"Because I promised them they would be able to play together, and now they can't."

"Mmmm," she sympathized.

"It's bad to break a promise," Edward said.

"Not in this case, it isn't," his mother told him firmly.

Rudy came by one Saturday morning when everyone except Edward and Spike and Rose had gone to Jason's soccer game. Edward and Spike and Rose liked cartoons better than they liked soccer. Edward liked his Game Boy better than soccer, too. He didn't mind staying home.

Rudy had twisted his knee at the beginning of the soccer season, so he wasn't playing, either.

He arrived at the door with Clifford perched on his shoulder. Clifford was facing backward, and his long tail was curled under Rudy's nose. It looked like a skinny, pinkish-white mustache. Edward couldn't help laughing when he saw it.

"Come on in, Rudy," Edward said. "I was just watching cartoons and playing with Spike and my Game Boy."

"What games do you have?" Rudy asked.

The boys sat down on the couch, careful to avoid sitting on Spike, who was sniffing in its corners and running along its back and arms.

"I have Jurassic Park and Mario Land and Metroid 2," Edward said. "Want to try?"

Rudy sat down next to Edward and picked up the Game Boy. He started to play Jurassic Park. Edward could tell Rudy was very good at the game, and he watched with admiration at how quickly Rudy won.

Clifford jumped off Rudy's shoulder and ran around on the back and the arms of the couch with Spike. Both boys concentrated on the Game Boy, and when they got tired of playing, they watched cartoons.

After a while, Rudy reached over and got Clifford

and put the rat back on his shoulder. "Well," he said to Edward, "see ya. Tell Jason to call me when he gets back from the game."

"Okay," said Edward, picking Spike up to put her back into her cage. "And tell Katherine 'hi' for us."

Rudy laughed. "Okay," he said, "I will. And next time I'll bring her over for a visit."

The rat cages were pushed close together on their shelf in the family room. And Spike and Rose often stood up on their hind legs, twitching and whiffling their rat noses at each other. Edward watched them. He could tell how much they wanted to play together. He was often tempted to take them out and let them play on the couch for just a few minutes. But he never did it. He knew that if you put a male and female rat together, even for a short time, you could find yourself with a whole litter of babies, and that some of those babies, no matter how much you liked them or wanted to keep them, would have to end up as boa brunch. And he knew that would make him feel even worse than disappointing Rose and Spike. So Edward did not give in to temptation. Not even one time. And he knew Jason didn't, either.

· · ·

Rats!

One rainy evening after dinner, Jason was doing his homework upstairs in the dining room so if he got stuck his parents could help him. Mr. Fraser was in the living room reading the newspaper. And Mrs. Fraser was sitting on the floor near the fireplace, adding some new specimens to her shell collection. Edward was downstairs with the rats. He played with Rose first and then he put him back into his cage. Then he went to take Spike out.

But when he looked into Spike's cage, he saw something that astonished him. He saw something coming out of Spike! It was a tiny something, smaller than Edward's thumb. It was hairless and pink, and its eye slits were tightly closed. It was a baby rat!

"Mom!" Edward screamed. *"Mom!"*

"What is it, Edward?" she called.

"Mom! Spike is having babies!"

"Edward, that's impossible," his mother called. "Spike has never been with a male rat. She can't have babies. Remember?"

Edward watched Spike's tiny pink hairless baby curl up next to its mother. And then he saw that Spike was going to give birth to another one.

"Remember, honey?" his mother called to him, patiently.

"Yes," he whispered. He remembered. But here

it came, the next baby. Smaller than Edward's thumb. Pink and bare. With its tiny eye slits squeezed shut.

Edward watched, rapt, breathing hard. Now he was glad nobody was there except him.

The babies squirmed close to Spike, pushing at her as if they were looking for something. Edward waited and watched. How many more babies would there be, he wondered. How long would it take them to come?

And he thought, what a clever rat Spike is, making these babies even though he and Jason had followed the rules perfectly and had never even once given in to the temptation to let her play with Rose.

Auntie Bea's Present

Great-aunt Beatrice couldn't remember birthdays, so she sent not-birthday presents to Jason and Edward once a year, whenever she felt like sending them.

One day, the boys came home from school to find a middle-sized box wrapped in brown paper and tied with string.

"It's from Great-aunt Beatrice, addressed to both of you," their mother told them.

"I can read," Jason reminded her as he read the mailing labels on the package.

"So can I read, sort of," Edward told her, as he pretended to read the labels on the package.

"Well, aren't you guys going to open it?" Mrs. Fraser asked eagerly.

"Sure," said Edward.

"Later," Jason said. "First I want a snack. I'm hungry."

"Don't you want to find out what's inside the package right away?" asked Mrs. Fraser. "I've been waiting all day long."

The boys knew from past experience that presents from Great-aunt Beatrice didn't have to be opened right away.

"Auntie never sends anything we want," Jason explained to his mother.

"But, Jason," she said, "you never know. This time, your Great-aunt Beatrice might have sent the best presents you boys have ever gotten!"

Mrs. Fraser gazed at the package almost as hungrily as Jason looked at the food in the refrigerator.

"It might be the present of your dreams," she told them. "Something you've always wanted but never thought of."

This got Edward's attention. "Yeah," he said softly, regarding the box with more interest. "It might be."

"Not if it comes from Great-aunt Beatrice," insisted Jason as he took out the leftover chicken and the chocolate milk.

"You never know," his mother said again.

"Jason, you never know," Edward repeated.

"So, shall we just open it and see?" asked Mrs. Fraser.

"You go ahead," Jason replied, looking at the comics from the morning paper and munching on a drumstick.

Edward's eyes were shining. "I'll open it," he said. "I have a feeling it might be a really good present this time."

"I have a feeling you're going to be disappointed," said Jason cheerfully.

Mrs. Fraser handed the scissors to Edward. He cut the string. Then he pulled away the brown paper and came to a box, gift-wrapped and tied with blue, gold, and white ribbons. "You have to admit, Jason," said Mrs. Fraser, "Auntie deserves an A-plus for wrapping."

Jason glanced at the box and nodded. Edward cut the fancy ribbon and carefully undid the pretty paper. His mother stood over him as he took off the top of a white box. "I love presents," she murmured happily.

"What's inside?" asked Jason.

"Tissue paper," answered Edward.

"See what's underneath," urged Mrs. Fraser.

Edward looked under the tissue paper and drew in his breath. "Wow!" he exclaimed.

That got Jason's attention. "What is it?" he wanted to know.

"Something very *red!*" Edward told him. Edward was an artist. He loved colors.

"What is it besides red?" Jason prompted.

"It's a sweater," Edward said. "A red, red sweater!"

Mrs. Fraser peered into the box. "It's two red, red sweaters," she said.

She held up one of the sweaters so Jason could see. It had long sleeves and buttons down the front. "Fancy cardigan sweaters!" Mrs. Fraser said, beaming.

"Try it on," she urged, holding one out to Jason. "I bet you'll look very handsome in this."

Jason washed his hands. He took the sweater from his mother and put it on. The color was clear and bright. The yarn was soft. It was the nicest sweater Jason had ever seen. Even though he hadn't been wanting a sweater, when he looked at himself in the mirror he saw that this sweater was special. He saw that the bright color did make him look handsome. "And it fits," he observed.

"Try yours on, Edward," Mrs. Fraser urged.

Edward was staring at the other sweater. Just feasting his eyes on the color made him feel happy. He hadn't even thought about wearing it. His mother helped him put it on.

The color looked good on Edward, too.

"And it doesn't fit," observed Jason.

He was right. The bottom of the sweater came halfway to Edward's knees. The sleeves hung down over his fingers.

"It sure doesn't," Edward said, holding out his sweater-covered hands.

"Not to worry!" Mrs. Fraser told him. "That's the great thing about a sweater. It doesn't have to really fit to look all right." Quickly, she folded the bottom of the sweater under. Then she rolled up the sleeves. "There!" she said, beaming. "See?"

Jason and Edward were doubtful.

"It's fine!" she assured them. "And such a brilliant color!"

Reminded about the color, Edward smiled. The color was what really mattered.

"Take off the sweaters, now, boys," Mrs. Fraser said. "These are too nice for everyday. I want you to save them for special occasions."

Jason thought that was too bad. He had planned to wear his sweater to school the next day.

But Edward didn't mind. He could spread the

103

sweater out on his bed and see beautiful red color. That would be every bit as good as wearing it.

"Boys, you forgot about the card," Mrs. Fraser called after Jason and Edward as they headed off to their rooms. Back they came.

The card was homemade by Great-aunt Beatrice. It showed stick-figure boys wearing bright red sweaters. It said, "Happy not-birthday to Jason and Edward, with love, your Ant Bee."

Mrs. Fraser handed the card to Jason. "Ant Bee," he read. "That same corny joke."

"What?" Edward wanted to know. "What's the joke?"

"See?" Mrs. Fraser showed him the card. "The right way for a relative is A-u-n-t instead of A-n-t. A-n-t is the insect, ant. And Auntie's name is spelled B-e-a, short for Beatrice, not B-e-e, like buzzzz."

Edward looked confused.

"It's a spelling joke," his mother explained. "See? Ant. Bee."

Edward stared hard at the letters. A-n-t, ant. He read ant! B-e-e, bee. He read bee!

"Ant! Bee!" he cried. "I can read!"

For once, Great-aunt Beatrice had sent truly wonderful gifts. Not only red sweaters that both boys liked, but also the first two words that Edward could really read.

"That's exactly what I meant," Mrs. Fraser told them. "That's why a package is so exciting. You just never know what might be inside."

The boys had to agree with her.

Once Edward could read "ant" and "bee," he caught on quickly. Almost overnight, he found he could read a lot of other words, too. Soon he could read every single word in his reading book at school, and his teacher jumped him from the Blue Jays to the Robins, from the bottom reading group to the top one, without even stopping at Sparrows.

"Who would have thought it would be Great-aunt Beatrice who would help Edward learn to read!" exclaimed Mrs. Fraser happily.

"A pretty darn good present, if you ask me," Mr. Fraser replied.

After school, Jason had soccer practice. He had piano lessons. He had homework.

Edward had free time.

"I'll be back," Edward said to Jason one day when their mother was out. Jason was doing long division.

"Where are you going?" he asked.

"Over to Emily's. To play."

"Play," Jason grumbled.

"Bye," said Edward.

Jason looked up. Edward was wearing his new sweater. "Edward, you're not supposed to wear that sweater to play in," Jason reminded his brother.

"I won't," said Edward. "I'll take it off while we play. I'll fold it up and put it over my handlebars."

"Edward," Jason said, "would you be doing this if Mom were home?"

Edward thought.

"Edward?"

"Well."

"Well, what?"

"Well, probably not," admitted Edward.

"Probably!" said Jason.

"Bye," said Edward.

Through the window of his room, Jason watched Edward flash up the driveway on his red bike, wearing his red sweater.

"Free time," said Jason, sighing. Then he went back to long division.

After long division, Jason studied his spelling words. Just as he was finishing, he saw Edward coming back.

Edward was walking his bike. He was crying. One sleeve of the red sweater was tangled in Edward's bicycle chain, which hung loose. The rest of the sweater was dragging on the ground.

Jason rushed outside to see if he could help.

Edward stood with tears running down his cheeks while Jason untangled the sweater. He held it up. It was torn, and it was covered with black grease.

"Mom's not back yet," Jason told Edward. "Put your bike away and meet me in my room." He rolled up the ruined sweater and hurried inside.

"How did this happen?" he asked Edward when he came in. "Stop crying and tell me."

Edward looked as if he was ready to cut loose and bawl. But Jason said firmly, "You haven't got time to cry right now, Edward."

Still, Edward couldn't talk. He was too upset.

"Did you take off the sweater when you got to Emily's?"

Edward shook his head yes.

"Did you fold it up and put it over your handlebars?"

Yes.

"And then?"

"And then Emily had to go, so I came home," explained Edward, sniffling.

"I meant and then what happened to the sweater?"

"I was all hot and sweaty from playing, so I tied it around my waist instead of putting it back on. And—and—the part that was hanging down got caught . . ." Edward was off again.

107

"In your bike chain," Jason said. Edward nodded.

"Mom is going to kill you," said Jason thoughtfully. Miserable, Edward nodded again.

"Unless . . ."

"Unless?" asked Edward.

"Well, unless she doesn't find out. Or at least unless she doesn't find out right away, while she still thinks these sweaters are such a big deal."

"They are such a big deal," Edward wailed.

"No, they aren't, Edward," Jason said kindly. "They're very nice. But they're just sweaters. And after a while she won't care about them so much. You don't care as much about stuff after you get used to it, do you?"

"Not really," Edward agreed.

"So after she gets used to seeing us looking handsome in our red sweaters, she won't care as much whether they're in perfect shape or not. And then you can tell her what happened. After all, you didn't do it on purpose," reasoned Jason.

"How is Mom going to get used to seeing us in our red sweaters when there's two of us and only one of them?" Edward asked, starting to cry again.

"Well," said Jason. "That part won't be easy. But I think I know how we can keep her from finding out, at least for a while."

After Jason told Edward his plan, and Edward

agreed to try it, Jason hid the torn sweater. Edward washed the dirt and tears off his face. And when their mother came home, she found both boys out in the driveway fixing the chain on Edward's bike.

The first occasion Edward and Jason had to deal with was their neighbor Elaine Abrams's sister's wedding.

The invitation came in the mail, addressed to "The Fraser Family."

"How nice!" Mrs. Fraser said. "We've all been invited to Jennifer Abrams's wedding. To the ceremony and to the party afterward."

"Jennifer Abrams is getting married?" said Jason, feeling a bit put out. Jennifer had been his favorite baby-sitter.

"So it would seem," his mother said, waving the invitation in his direction.

"Getting married," Mr. Fraser said when he came home. "Little Jenny Abrams."

"She's getting married in the park and the party will be there at the recreation center after the ceremony," Mrs. Fraser told him. "I guess it's a modern wedding."

"Why?" Edward wanted to know.

"Because it's taking place in a park," his mother told him.

Mr. Fraser didn't like to get dressed up. "In the park," he said. "Good. Then I guess I won't have to wear a tie."

"Not wear a tie to a wedding!" Mrs. Fraser exclaimed. "What can you be thinking?"

"I was thinking how nice it would be to be comfortable at a wedding," said Mr. Fraser.

Mrs. Fraser liked to get dressed up. "A wedding is always a dressy occasion," she said. "Besides, how can I wear a fancy dress if you don't have a tie on?"

"You could just wear it," suggested Mr. Fraser.

Mrs. Fraser shook her head. "Even if the wedding is in the park," she explained, "everyone will still get dressed up. A wedding is not your everyday thing, after all."

Mr. Fraser shrugged. He knew he would wear a tie to the wedding.

"Really," Mrs. Fraser tried comforting him, "you'll see. All the men will have on ties."

"What about the boys?" Edward wanted to know. He and Jason didn't have ties.

"The boys will be dressed up, too, of course," his mother answered. "You boys can wear your new red sweaters!"

· · ·

110

When the day of the wedding came, Edward wore a new red sweater. And Jason decided to wear his navy-blue blazer jacket from the year before. "I've almost grown out of it," he explained to his mother. "This is probably the last time I'll be able to squeeze myself into this jacket. I want to wear it one more time."

"I didn't realize you liked your blazer so much," his puzzled mother said.

"I do," Jason assured her. "I always have."

The next dress-up occasion Jason and Edward had to deal with was going out to dinner with their parents.

"We're taking you boys out to dinner at Rinaldi's, a fancy Italian restaurant," their father told them.

"Why?" asked Edward.

"For fun," his mother said.

"We have more fun at home," Jason told her.

"You have to learn how to behave—and have fun—away from home," Mrs. Fraser said. "So get out your manners and your red sweaters, and let's get ready to go."

This time, Jason wore the red sweater. Edward wore Jason's blazer, even though it was big on him.

"Jason just gave it to me," Edward explained to

his mother, holding out his hands so she could fold up the sleeves. "He outgrew it, and now I get to have it. I want to wear it right away."

"I didn't realize you liked Jason's blazer so much," his puzzled mother said.

"I do," Edward assured her. "I always have."

The next occasion Jason and Edward had to deal with was the Christmas-card photograph.

"This year, I want to send a card with a picture of you two handsome boys on it," their mother told them. "Get showered, comb your hair, and put on fresh pants and shirts," she said, getting out her camera and her tripod and a roll of film. "I want you to sit in the living room in front of the fireplace. I've decorated it with pine branches and hung up the Christmas stockings. It will make a perfect background."

The boys could see their mother meant business. Christmas cards were on her mind. They headed for the shower.

"And I want both of you wearing a red sweater!" she called after them. "A red sweater is the perfect thing for a Christmas card."

The boys raced to Jason's room and closed the door.

"Now what will we do?" said Edward.

"Nothing," said Jason.

"Nothing?"

"The jig is up," Jason said. "We have to face the music."

"What are you talking about?" Edward wanted to know.

"There's nothing we can do this time," Jason explained. "Mom wants us each in a red sweater for the Christmas-card picture. Red, you know, for Christmas. We won't be able to convince her to let one of us wear a blue blazer this time."

"And I guess we both have to be in the picture," said Edward.

"Of course we do," Jason agreed. "Mom and Dad aren't going to send out Christmas cards showing just one of us."

"So there's nothing we can do."

"Nothing."

"We have to tell her."

"We have to confess."

"Mom will be furious."

"She'll be disappointed."

"About the Christmas card."

"And about the sweater."

They regarded each other. "No way out," Jason said, shrugging.

Then Edward had an idea.

The boys showered, combed their hair, and put on fresh clothes.

When their mother called, "Are you boys almost ready?" they answered, "In a minute, Mom."

Then they came into the living room together.

Mrs. Fraser turned the camera toward the doorway so she could take an unposed picture of the boys when they walked into the room. She peered through the viewfinder and focused the lens.

Looking through the camera, this is what she saw: she saw Jason and Edward walking side by side and step in step. Jason had his right arm in one arm of a red sweater. He had his left arm around Edward's shoulders.

Edward had his left arm in one arm of the same red sweater. He had his right arm around Jason's waist. Both boys had serious expressions on their faces.

Their mother snapped a picture. Then she waited while her sons, step in step, walked toward her. She could tell they had a story to relate, and she was very interested to find out what it was.

But she could also tell that whatever the story was, the thing they would all be interested in, in the end, would be the funny photograph of Jason and Edward that she had just snapped.